Contents

Lizards
and
Snakes

**Rod Theodorou
and Carole Telford**

Rigby

Introduction

Lizards are **reptiles**. They are **cold-blooded**. Lizards have to warm up by lying in the sun each day. Most lizards have **scales** covering their skin. There are 3,000 different kinds of lizards.

Snakes are reptiles, too. They have long, thin bodies and no legs. Like lizards, snakes are covered with scales and are cold-blooded. There are 2,400 kinds of snakes.

Size

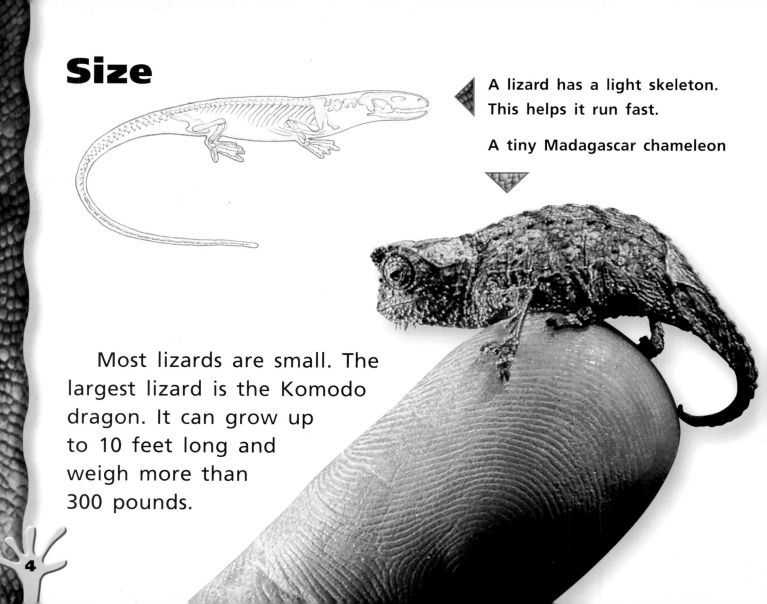

A lizard has a light skeleton. This helps it run fast.

A tiny Madagascar chameleon

Most lizards are small. The largest lizard is the Komodo dragon. It can grow up to 10 feet long and weigh more than 300 pounds.

4

A reticulated python

There are many sizes of snakes. The longest snake is the reticulated python, which can grow up to 30 feet. The heaviest snake is the anaconda, weighing up to 300 pounds.

Human beings have 12 pairs of ribs. Snakes have hundreds!

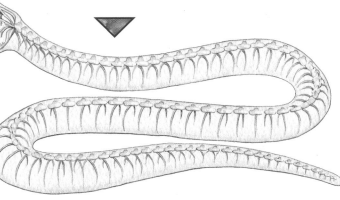

Habitat

Lizards live all over the world, but mostly in hot places. They live on the ground and in trees. Lizards that live in cool places have to spend a lot of time in the sun.

The marine iguana is unusual because it lives by the sea.

The giant anaconda lives in rivers in South America.

Snakes live in every part of the world, too. Most snakes live in hot places and on the ground. In cooler places, snakes, like lizards, have to lie in the sun almost all the time.

Senses

Lizards have very good eyesight. Chameleons can move their eyes in different directions when looking for insects. Lizards can "taste" the air in the same way that people smell things. Lizards flick out their tongues to sense what is going on around them.

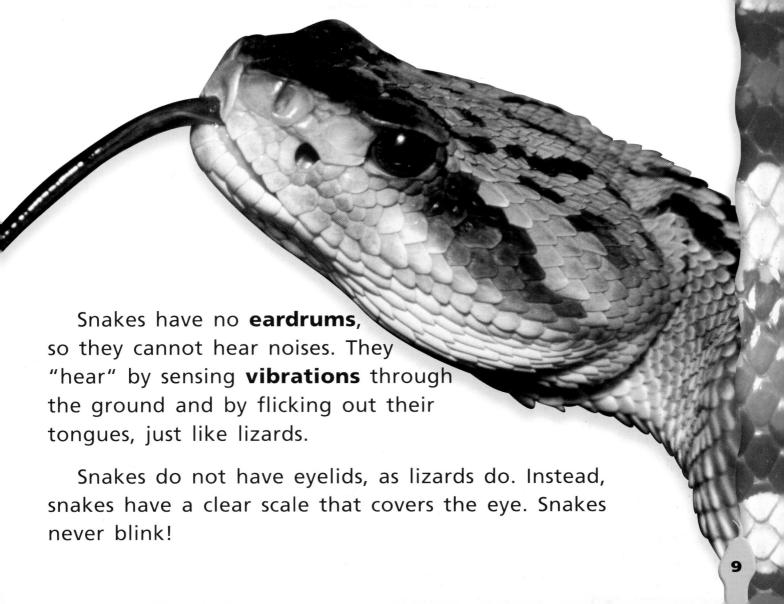

Snakes have no **eardrums**, so they cannot hear noises. They "hear" by sensing **vibrations** through the ground and by flicking out their tongues, just like lizards.

Snakes do not have eyelids, as lizards do. Instead, snakes have a clear scale that covers the eye. Snakes never blink!

Staying Hidden

Many lizards need to be able to stay hidden, either to avoid enemies or to stalk their **prey**. Some are the same color as the sand they live on. Others are the same color as the leaves or the bark of the trees they live in.

The horned lizard is hard to see among the stones and sand.

The skin of a Gaboon viper has a pattern that makes it very hard to find in the leaves.

A MacMahon's viper is buried in the desert sand.

Snakes are often the same color as their surroundings, too. Sometimes their skin looks like sand, gravel, or leaves.

Moving

Lizards are fast runners and good climbers. Gecko lizards have special feet that can grip any surface—even glass!

The flying lizard lives in trees. It glides from tree to tree by stretching out special flaps of skin on its side.

Many snakes move from side to side in "s" shapes. This pushes them along the ground and up trees. Snakes ripple the muscles along their spines and "walk" on their hundreds of ribs.

Food

Lizards eat mostly insects. Some lizards, like the green iguana, also eat plants. Big lizards, like the Komodo dragon, eat meat.

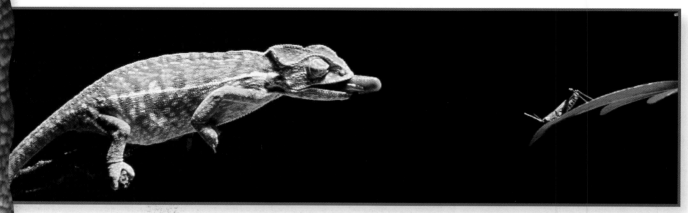

A chameleon flicks out its incredibly long tongue to trap an insect.

All snakes are meat eaters. They cannot chew, so they have to swallow their food whole. They have a very loose-hinged jaw so they can open their mouths extra wide.

An African egg-eating snake enjoys a meal.

Hunting

Lizards that hunt insects sneak up on their prey and then pounce and bite them. Some lizards, like the gecko lizard, are nocturnal—they hunt at night.

A chameleon sneaks up on an unsuspecting fly.

All snakes have sharp teeth. Some snakes also have fangs that can inject **venom**, a poison, into their prey. Other snakes kill their prey by squeezing. They squeeze until the prey can no longer breathe, and it dies.

The fangs of a venomous red-diamond rattlesnake

Defense

Lizards have many enemies, including snakes. Lizards avoid being eaten by hiding or by running away fast.

The blue-tongued lizard sticks out its tongue to scare off enemies.

The Australian frilled lizard raises its frill to scare its enemies.

Snakes are hunted by other animals, such as birds, pigs, and even other snakes. They can often avoid capture by hiding and staying still.

The rattlesnake warns off enemies by shaking its tail, causing loose scales at the end to rattle.

The hognose snake pretends to be dead if it is disturbed!

Babies

Some female lizards lay soft, leathery eggs in a hole in the ground. The eggs are warmed by the sun. When the eggs hatch, the mother does not look after the babies. Baby lizards have to look after themselves.

An iguana lays up to 75 eggs at a time.

Baby snakes hatch from their eggs.

Like lizards, some snakes lay eggs, while others have live young. Most snakes lay 6 to 30 eggs at a time. After laying their eggs, most female snakes leave them.

Comparison Chart

Lizards

- four legs
- eat insects or plants
- pounce on prey
- run fast
- most are small
- good eyesight
- have eyelids

- reptiles
- cold-blooded
- scales cover skin
- many different kinds
- live all over the world
- most live in hot places
- blend in with surroundings
- climb trees

Snakes

- no legs
- eat meat
- bite or squeeze prey
- slither
- different sizes
- sense vibrations through the ground
- no eyelids

Glossary

I may be cold-blooded, but I have a warm heart!

cold-blooded having a body temperature that is controlled by the environment

eardrums a thin piece of skin in the ear that helps animals hear

prey an animal that is hunted by another animal for food

reptiles animals that are cold-blooded and covered in scales; snakes, lizards, crocodiles, turtles, and tortoises are all reptiles

scales hard, thin plates that cover and protect the skin

venom poison

vibrations shaking movements

Index